Chinook's Christmas

By Christopher Staviski

Illustrated By Lilith Valebali

ISBN-10: 0692139362
ISBN-13: 978-0692139363 (Custom Universal)

Illustrator: Lilith Valebali
Editor: Jon Sorensen
Aloha Chinook Logo Text Created By: Juwaun Mccrary
Chinook's Tales Logo Created By: Juwaun Mccrary
Formatting by: Chrissy at Indie Publishing Group

Second printing March 2019

"Well son, welcome to Kodiak Island," the pilot says. "You know why they call it Kodiak Island, doncha?"

"No sir," Zack replies.

"Cuz of the bears. But, your Uncle Jay keeps an eye on them, so you'll be okay," he says as he points to the shore. "That's him at the beginning of the pier."

"Welcome to your new home," Uncle Jay says. "You'll want to stay close by until you get use to the Alaskan woods, and our only neighbor is a couple of miles away. You'll need to watch out for bears. And, you don't want to run into Kinak, he's a great big bear with a large scar on his face."

Zack looks to the woods and his eyes grow wide with curiosity. "I'll be careful sir," Zack says.

"Good," Uncle Jay replies, "and I'm sorry for the loss of your mom and dad. Also, call me "Uncle Jay." I'm your family now."

Zack whispers to himself, "It's not the same."

KODIAK WILDLIFE
FOUNDATION

The next day, Zack decides to explore the woods by his new home. But, he wandered too far in and got lost.

He turns to go back home and runs right into Kinak, the largest Kodiak bear in all of Alaska. And, Kinak is mad.

Zack runs as fast as he can and hides
from Kinak behind a log. He waits there
until Kinak gets bored and leaves.

Zack is lost, but he wanders the woods until he finds a small cabin.

Outside the cabin is Anik, a local Inuit native. He says, "You must be Zack, Jay's nephew."

Zack says, "Yes sir, do you know him?"

"Of course I do," he responds. "You look lost. I'll take you home."

But before they can leave, a puppy pokes her head out from behind the front door.

The puppy runs out of the cabin and jumps on Zack, knocking him to the ground. He laughs out loud as the puppy licks his face.

Anik laughs and says, "This is Chinook, and she is one of the puppies from my old dog Silla. She is a Siberian Husky and her name comes from the warm winds that flow down from the mountains, which signifies the end of winter. She likes you, so you can have her."

Zack and Chinook become inseparable. They do everything together, like; play catch. Run. Tug of war. And, enjoy being around each other.

Months pass by and Chinook is no longer a puppy. Zack, Uncle Jay, and Chinook are enjoying the evening in Kodiak City.

They see their friend Anik and his daughter Ila. Ila's daughter Alasie gives Zack an Eskimo kiss by pressing her nose against his.

"You are Zack," Alasie says, "I'm Alasie and I'm giving you an Eskimo kiss.

Actually, we call it a kunik and it is my people's way of saying if you're Mister Jay's

family then you are my family."

Ila asks, "How about we bring Alasie by tomorrow to play with Zack?"

Uncle Jay says, " Of course, that will be great."

The next day, Alasie and Zack play with Chinook. Zack asks her, "Where is your dad? I didn't see him yesterday."

Alasie says, "He's gone just like your parents. I miss him, but he made sure that I had my angels to watch over me in my mom and my grampa. Your parent's made sure you had an angel to watch over you in your Uncle Jay. Or maybe, Chinook is your angel."

"Maybe," Zack says.

"Chinook is getting big," Alasie says, "I bet you can't pick her up."

Zack responds, "I can too. I can pick her up and throw her in the air and catch her."

Zack picks up Chinook and throws her in the air.

And she flies. Furry wings spring from her body and flaps like a bird. Zack and Alasie stare in disbelief.

Alasie says, "She...she...she can fly!"

She can fly. She flies higher and faster than the biggest eagle around.

Zack says to Alasie, "We cannot tell anyone that Chinook can fly. Not Uncle Jay, or even your mom and grampa."

"But my grampa probably already knows," Alasie says, "he had her as a puppy."

Zack says, "I know, but we shouldn't say anything to be sure. I don't want anyone getting scared and taking her away from me."

"I understand," she responds. "You are walking too close to the edge of the river. You'll fall in if you are not careful."

But Zack was not careful and fell into the roaring waters. The water whips him quickly down the river.

Chinook and Alasie run after him, but they cannot catch up. Alasie notices the big scary waterfall ahead of Zack. She screams, "Watch out for that waterfall!"

Zack's eyes grow wide with fear as he looks at the waterfall and yells "Chinook!!!"

Zack falls over the waterfall and drops straight towards the rocks at the bottom.
But, Chinook grabs him by his ankle and safely takes him to the shore.

Uncle Jay, Zack, and Chinook walk the streets of Kodiak two days before Christmas and they meet Santa Claus. Santa says, "Hi Zack. What do you want for Christmas?"

Zack smiles and says, "I don't need anything, Santa. I have Chinook."

"Yes you do," Santa says as he pets her head. "After all, she is your Christmas angel."

It is Christmas Eve. Uncle Jay gathers Zack and Chinook outside. He says, "We will have to wait to decorate the Christmas tree. Kinak the bear is not hibernating, which means he is hungry and looking for food. Stay close to the cabin until I find him."

Chinook flies around the yard while Uncle Jay is gone. Suddenly, Uncle Jay arrives back at the cabin. He gets out of his truck and points to the sky. He is shocked to see Chinook flying.

Unfortunately, Uncle Jay knows that they can't keep a flying dog and takes Chinook away to give her back to Anik.

Zack is upset and runs away into the forest.

Zack runs to the edge of a very high cliff. He hears a growl behind him. He turns around and sees Kinak staring at him, and he looks hungry. Zack screams "HELP!!!"

Chinook hears Zack's scream and breaks the leash from Uncle Jay's hand. She flaps her wings as hard and fast as she can to get to Zack.

She dives like a speeding rocket and slams into Kinak, causing him to fall over the edge of the cliff.

Kinak is dazed and stumbles to his cave.
He knows that it is time for him to hibernate.

"Merry Christmas!" Yells Uncle Jay, Alasie, Ila, and Anik.

Zack and Chinook wake up surprised to see everyone.

"We forgot to decorate the tree yesterday due to all of the excitement," says Uncle Jay.

Zack and the rest are outside by the large tree in the yard. Zack says to Chinook, "Play catch."

Chinook flies around the tree as Zack and Uncle Jay throw decorations to her to put on the tree.

Ila is surprised that Chinook can fly.

Zack looks at everyone holding hands and says to himself, "I thought that family without my parents is not the same, but I was wrong. I miss my parents and always will, but here is my family now and I love them. And, Chinook looks out for me."

Zack looks at his new family and proudly says, "Merry Christmas."